Giant Love

The Magical Midlife Series

By

Rose Bak

Table of Contents

Copyright

About This Book

A giant walks into a bar, and leaves with a succubus…

Despite being a human, Dianne grew up with the stories that she comes from a long line of female demons. She doesn't believe the family lore – at least until the day a huge football player tracks her down, claiming that she called to him in his dreams.

Nephilim Elijah is used to being the biggest guy in the room. He's turned his size into a profitable career in American football, but the giant has always felt like something was missing. When a curvy beauty starts haunting his dreams, he's determined to track her down. The minute their eyes meet, he knows that he's finally found his fated mate.

He's ready to move to Greysden and start a family with her. Unfortunately, Dianne's got other ideas, and falling in love is not in her plan. Neither is being a mother…

"Giant Feelings" is a steamy midlife paranormal romantic comedy featuring a woman finding her supernatural side, a lovable giant who takes things a little too literally, and nosy small-town matchmakers determined to help them find their happily ever after.

About the "Magical Midlife" series: Just outside the shifter town of Greysden sits Rosewater Manor, a place shrouded in magic. The Rosewater women and their friends all have special gifts, although sometimes they're a bit glitchy. At least until they find true love…

Join My Mailing List

Join Rose Bak's mailing list at bit.ly/RoseBakNewsletter[2]. You'll get a free book and be the first to hear about all the latest releases and special sales.

Dedication

For everyone who believes in magic. I do too.

Dianne

"Well, there's something you don't see every day."

I turned to look in the direction that my friends Meri and Pepper were staring.

The two sisters looked very much alike but couldn't be more different. Meri was a quiet yet impish psychic while her sister Pepper was loud, brash, and had only recently come into her magical powers as a witch.

We'd been enjoying a quiet after-work happy hour until all hell broke loose. Across the bar Ben Murphy, a bear shifter who was also the owner of this establishment, dangled a fox shifter upside down by his feet. Well, his paws.

"Don't disrespect my mate again!" the bear shifter growled. "I'll gut you."

Marie, the woman who worked behind the bar, growled in annoyance and leapt over the counter to give her mate a hard jab in the ribs.

"Let him down, Gentle Ben. I was handling it."

Ben dropped the fox shifter to the floor, and the smaller man slunk towards the door, racing out just as someone came in. I recognized the familiar shape of Preston Rutherford the third, Meri's mate. He was my boss, as well as my friend.

I had worked for Preston for fifteen years back in New York City. But when he'd been attacked by rogue werewolves and turned into a shifter last year, an entire new world had opened up to him. Like most humans, he had no idea that there was a completely different world operating alongside the human world, one filled with animal shifters, vampires, and other supernatural creatures.

Becoming a shifter in midlife wasn't an easy transition for Preston. After he had a shifting malfunction that left him naked and confused in

Central Park, our friend and colleague Duncan, also a wolf shifter, had convinced Preston to move to Greysden.

Duncan had grown up here, and he figured the best place for Preston to learn about his new dual nature was in a town full of shifters. And demons. And witches. Really Greysden welcomed everyone, even full humans, although they were definitely in the minority.

People had thought Preston was crazy for leaving New York City for some tiny town in Colorado, but I'd jumped at the chance to follow him. After so many years living crammed in a shoebox apartment in the city, I'd appreciated the opportunity to finally have some space and a yard where I could garden.

I'd pretended to resist, of course, in order to encourage Preston to make it worth my while to move with him.

"Hi all," Preston greeted us, dropping a kiss on the top of Meri's head.

The younger psychic had been really good for Preston. Although I liked him a lot, my boss had always been a bit spoiled, the quintessential rich boy. But Meri had whipped him into shape, and the changing of his priorities had only been for the better.

"Hi boss," I greeted him.

Preston rolled his eyes. He hated it when I called him that, which was precisely why I did it.

With the fox drama over, Marie bustled over to our table to take our drink orders. She was a pretty she-wolf about my age.

"What happened with the fox?" Pepper asked.

"Oh, apparently he has a foot fetish. He asked me to take off my shoes and let him suck my toes, so Ben got all growly about it." She rolled her eyes. "Like I didn't work here for nearly twenty years before he moved to town. I've dealt with way worse than a kinky fox before."

The door opened and we all glanced in that direction. Whoever was coming in was massive – he totally blocked all the light. We watched as he ducked to get in the door, despite it being a bear-shifter sized entry. The giant man stepped inside, his eyes swinging across the space.

He was tall and broad with mile-wide shoulders, massive biceps, a broad chest, and legs that looked wider than tree trunks. Judging by his trim waist and flat abdomen, there wasn't an ounce of fat on the guy.

I looked up – way up – to see dark hair, a short, cropped beard across a square jaw, and the most beautiful brown eyes I'd ever seen. His gaze snapped to me, and a look of pure joy crossed his handsome face.

He made a beeline across the bar, pushing people out of the way and staring at me the entire time. He stopped in front of our table. Goddess, this dude had to be close to seven feet tall. And almost that wide.

"Mate! I found you!"

His voice was deep and grumbly. It did funny things to my insides.

"Oh. My. Goddess!" Pepper's voice interrupted my thoughts, full of exasperation. "Why does this keep happening to me? It's like I'm a mate magnet for everyone except myself. I'm going to be alone forever!"

Pepper's desire to find a mate of her own was only surpassed by her annoyance that she seemed to be nearby while everyone else in town found their fated mates – whether they wanted to or not.

"Mine!"

I looked over my shoulder to make sure that the giant man wasn't talking to someone else. Nope, no one was behind me. He was definitely referring to me. Crap, this was bad. If there was one thing I didn't want at this stage of my life, it was a mate. I was happily single and unlike my friend Pepper, I'd never longed for a mate, supernatural or otherwise. And closing in on forty in two years, I figured I'd dodged that bullet.

"Mate." He said again, staring at me with an intensity that made me want to climb him like a tree. Until I remembered that I didn't want a mate. I straightened my spine and fixed him with a stern look.

"I think you're mistaken, buddy. I am not your mate."

I imbued my voice with as much conviction as I could muster, even as I knew in the depths of my soul that the guy was right. I could feel the mate bond as well as he could. I was just determined to ignore it.

"It is you, I saw you. You called to me in my dreams, little mate. You brought me here."

I flinched. I'd always suspected I had a bit of the supernatural inside me, but I'd always figured it was just latent. Sure, I could tell a supe from a normal, but other than that, I was for all intents and purposes a human.

Or so I'd thought. Now I knew the truth: my demon side had finally been activated, and apparently I'd called myself a mate.

I took a deep breath and looked around at my friends who were watching the scene with avid interest.

"Fun fact you might not know about me. My mother is a succubus."

Elijah

I looked down at the curvy beauty sitting at the table, scarcely able to believe my luck. She was perfect for me. My mate had long blonde hair and a soft and womanly figure that I couldn't wait to explore – a perfect hourglass. Her eyes were brown, and her skin was pale and creamy.

"What's a succubus?" A man sitting at her table asked.

I sniffed subtly. He smelled like dog. Probably a wolf shifter. I knew this town at the base of the Colorado mountains had been settled by wolves and built up as a haven for shifters. I would break him in half for sitting too close to my mate, but I could tell by the way he was touching the younger woman with the brown and blonde hair that he had his own mate, and thus he was no threat to me.

"A succubus is a female demon who was thought to seduce men in their sleep," the woman with the multicolored hair explained.

"That's just a rumor the religious people made up to disempower strong females," my mate tossed over her shoulder. "Prophetic dreams are not the same as seducing men."

"How did I not know this about you, Dianne?" the man asked.

Ah, my mate's name was Dianne. It suited her.

"I thought it was latent. My mother was…is…a succubus-type demon, and she always swore that my father was a human," my mate explained. "I sometimes dream about the future, but honestly my dreams have never been more reliable than anyone else's."

"No wonder you didn't bat an eye when I was turned into a wolf," the man continued. "You already knew about the supernatural world."

Growing bored with the conversation, I pointed at my mate. "Come."

Her eyes flashed as she jumped out of her chair and slammed her hands onto her hips. She was dressed professionally in a snug-fitting navy blue pencil skirt that hugged her hips, and a lighter blue button down blouse that gave just a hint of her generous cleavage. Although she was tall for a woman and wearing shoes with heels, she only came up to my chest. Of course, I was taller than the average human, thanks to my Nephilim blood.

"Excuse you?" my mate said to me. "Come? I'm not a dog."

I looked at her in confusion. What was the problem?

"You're my mate. We must go and claim each other now."

"No we mustn't," she snapped. "You have a lot of nerve, buddy."

"Elijah. My name is Elijah."

The man at the table snapped his fingers. "Oh, that's why you look familiar, you're Tank Thomas, aren't you?"

I didn't even spare the wolf a glance. I had no time for my fans right now, not when I'd finally found my mate.

"Yes, I am."

"Tank Thomas?" Dianne asked.

I noticed that she squished her tiny little nose as she was thinking. It was adorable.

"Why does that sound familiar?" she asked.

"He played defense for the New York Giants," the man explained. "You would have heard a lot about him when we lived in New York. No player could get past him."

"You played for the Giants? That seems appropriate," another woman at the table snickered.

"I am a giant, I'm half Nephilim," I confirmed. "Both of my parents had Nephilim blood."

"I'd hate to see how big you'd be if you were a full blooded Nephilim," the woman said.

I didn't spare her a glance. All of my focus was on my mate. I'd been waiting for forty years to meet her, and I didn't want to waste another second without claiming her.

"You called me, and I came for you, Dianne. Now we will seal the mate bond as the fates intended."

My mate's mouth dropped open and the beast in me imagined her mouth open for another reason.

"If I called you – and that's a big IF – it was an accident," she objected. "Totally a wrong number. Now run along and find someone who actually wants a mate."

I heaved a sigh. Clearly my mate was going to play hard to get. Without another word, I grabbed her by the waist and hauled her over my shoulder like a sack of potatoes. She made a squeak as the air left her lungs. Everything inside me settled as I banded one arm around my mate's bare thighs, my skin touching hers.

"Hey! Put me down, asshole!"

She gave me a good punch right over my left kidney. My mate was strong. She'd have to be. My people had big babies. I lightly smacked her shapely ass.

"Be good."

She gasped in outrage and paused for a full ten seconds before resuming her struggle. "You don't get to talk to me like that!"

I kept my hand on her butt and I could feel the energy arcing between us even through the fabric. It was like every cell in my body was focused on her to the extent that I wasn't aware of anything else in the bar. Anything else in the world faded, other than the sensation of that sweet curve underneath my hand. I wondered if she felt it too, because suddenly she became very still.

Turning, I headed towards the door with Dianne still over my shoulder. I heard one of her friends call, "Have fun with your new mate!"

The words caused her to remember her predicament and start to struggle again. We reached the door, and a dark-haired man came through, looking at us curiously.

"Hey Dianne. Found your mate, I see. Congratulations."

"What is wrong with people in this town?" she hissed. "Duncan, help me."

The man chuckled. "You've been here around the supes long enough to know that resistance is futile. You might as well save yourself the trouble and accept the gift the fates have sent you."

"I want to send my gift back," she wailed as I shouldered past the man and exited the bar.

I took off up the street at a fast pace, my mate jostling a bit on my shoulder.

"Where are you taking me?" she asked my back.

"I have an Airbnb close to here," I told her. "We will go there to begin our mating."

"I'm not mating with you," she protested. "This is kidnapping! I could have you arrested."

This close I could smell her arousal. My mate was protesting, but I was one hundred percent sure that her panties were wet for me right now. She might resist, but she would not resist for long. I was sure of it.

Dianne

I couldn't believe this was happening to me. I was torn between sheer panic and a girlish thrill at the way this dude was carrying me like I weighed nothing. I'd swung between a size fourteen and a size sixteen my entire life, depending on how dedicated I was to dieting, but this guy made me feel...small.

Mind you, I was perfectly fine with how I looked. I exercised regularly, making me comfortable in my own skin, and I'd worked hard on my self-confidence in my younger years. But the sensation of being petite was a new one that I kind of liked.

Speaking of liking things, I had a birds eye view of Elijah's muscled ass and holy mother of all things muscular, it was a work of art. Staring at his ass took my mind off the way that I could feel his giant hand burning through my skirt like a brand on my own ass. My entire body was vibrating with awareness, my blood racing with excitement, telling me that both of our instincts were one hundred percent correct. This giant guy was my fated mate.

That didn't mean I needed to accept it. I wasn't a slave to my hormones or whatever part of my brain was tied to my succubus ancestors. At least I didn't think I was.

We got to a cottage a couple of blocks away from the bar, and Elijah paused at the door. A few seconds later it opened with a click.

"Put me down!" I demanded again as he stepped inside.

This time he listened, sliding me slowly – oh so slowly – down his body. He stepped back, his huge body blocking the front door, and I tried not to panic at the sensation of being trapped. Despite his caveman tactics, I honestly didn't think this guy would hurt me. Adjusting the skirt that had slid dangerously high on my thighs, I started pacing.

"I need to know what's going on. Tell me everything that led to you showing up here today," I instructed. "You're not from here, right?"

"I live in New York."

"How did you hear about Greysden?" I asked.

"You came to me in my dreams," he explained. "Every night for weeks you asked me to come to you. Then last night you finally showed me an image of a sign. It said 'Welcome to Greysden' so I knew this was where you were. I would have come here sooner if you had not waited to share that part."

"You understand that wasn't me, right?"

He shook his head. "It was you, Dianne. I saw you there and heard your voice, clear as day."

"Well if it was me, it was my subconscious. I have no memory of that."

The minute the words were out of my mouth I had a flash. I'd been dreaming of a large, dark-haired man off and on for a while now. It wasn't uncommon for me to have recurring dreams, so I hadn't thought too much about it. But maybe...

Maybe it was this guy? Is this how the succubus thing worked? I really needed to call my mother – if I could track her down. She'd give it to me straight – assuming she was sober. I didn't have any other living female relatives to ask, unfortunately.

"We will claim each other now," he said firmly.

"We will NOT claim each other now," I corrected. "I don't even know you."

Not that I'd ever been opposed to the occasional one-night-stand – especially with a dude as hot as this one—but I knew instinctively that this would not be the guy to try that with.

"We will get to know each other then, and when you feel more comfortable we will mate."

"Do you say anything that's not an order?" I snapped. "Because I gotta tell you, I am NOT the woman to boss around."

"Only in the bedroom?" he guessed.

I felt my face heat up as I had a flash of him ordering me to kneel down and suck his cock. Oh my Goddess, what was wrong with me? One corner of his mouth quirked up into a smirk, letting me know he'd read my thoughts on my face. Or at least the gist of them. It made me want to punch him.

"How about we talk for a few minutes so you can see that this is all a mistake, then I have to jet."

"Jet?" He looked confused.

"Leave."

"I do not like this idea." He had a very deliberate way of speaking, as if English wasn't his first language, though I didn't detect any trace of an accent.

I pointed to the overstuffed gray couch in the center of the room. It gave the living room a homey focal point, the space perfect for entertaining.

"Sit."

He sat in the middle of the couch, and I deliberately lowered myself into the matching armchair across from the couch. Without a word, Elijah got up, picked me up, and brought me back to the couch, sitting me on the cushion next to him.

"Hey!" I protested, scrambling to the far edge of the cushion to put some space between us. I turned sideways with my back pressed against the arm of the couch, bringing one knee up onto the cushion so I could face him – and have a barrier between us.

"What is wrong, mate?" He looked confused at my reaction.

"Quit picking me up like that, damn it. It's very rude. Now, where are you from?"

"I told you, New York."

"No, I mean, where were you born."

He looked confused. "New York."

"I thought I detected...an accent or something."

"I had a speech impediment growing up," he explained. "Speech therapy taught me how to speak in this manner. It becomes more pronounced when I feel strong emotions."

I felt like a total asshole. "I'm so sorry, I had no idea."

"It's okay. Both of my brothers had the same problem. Our mother said there were too many of us to get a word in edgewise and that is why we all struggled to speak."

"Too many of you?"

"We are triplets."

I reared back. "Oh my Goddess, there are three of you?" At his nod I asked, "Are they all your size?"

He shook his head. "My brothers are larger. Mama says I'm the runt of the litter."

I didn't even know what to say to that, so I moved on with my questions.

"You played football I heard. I assume you're too old for that now?" He looked to be about my age.

"I am forty, little mate. I have retired from the NFL so now I coach football."

"Of course you do. Is that your full-time gig?"

He nodded.

"What was your major in college?"

"I was drafted to the NFL out of high school, so I never went to college."

"Um. What interests do you have?"

"Football."

"And? What else?"

"Shows about football."

"What do you read then?" I asked, desperately trying to figure out why fate would have matched us with each other. "If you say books about football I swear I'm going to scream."

When he remained silent I prodded, "Why aren't you answering me?"

"I don't want you to scream again."

"So let me get this straight: the sum total of your life experience and your interests is football. Is that right?"

"There is one other thing that I am interested in."

"What's that?"

"My new mate."

Elijah

I had the feeling that I was disappointing my mate. Clearly she did not love football as much as I did, her one fault so far. But I knew many people whose mate had different interests from then. I remembered Mama telling us boys that when we were with a woman we should show interest in what was important to her. I should quiz her as she quizzed me.

"What is important to you, little mate?" I asked.

Her nose scrunched up again as she considered my question.

"My job, obviously."

"What is your job?" I asked. Clearly it was something in an office, based on her outfit.

"I'm the personal assistant to Preston Rutherford the third, the CEO of Rutherford Industries."

I must have looked confused because she added, "They're a worldwide corporation that works primarily in manufacturing, and exports. That was my boss Rutherford at the table, the one who called you Tank."

"Ah, the wolf."

"Yeah."

"What else are you interested in?" I asked politely instead of ripping her clothes off and rutting into her like a beast like my instincts were telling me.

"Well, I like reading. Musicals. Hiking. Yoga. Oh, and I like my cat."

"You have a pet feline?" I clarified.

"Yes." Dianne's face turned soft as she smiled affectionately. "His name is Mr. Fluffers, and he's the cutest little guy in the world. I love him so much."

I stared at her, transfixed. I knew it was ridiculous to be jealous of a cat, but right now I wanted nothing more than for her to look at me with the obvious devotion that she felt for her feline.

"I will endeavor not to eat him then," I teased.

Her face took on a look of horror. "What? Why would you eat him?"

"Some demons eat small prey."

"Mr. Fluffers is not your small prey." She sounded indignant.

I placed my hand on her arm to calm her, once again feeling that tingling sensation where we touched.

"I was joking, mate. I will not eat your feline. They are much too small to be more than an appetizer anyway."

She looked at me suspiciously. "Okay then. Maybe try to crack a smile when you make a joke."

This wasn't going as well as I hoped. When Dianne called to me in my dreams, I'd assumed that she'd be excited to see me. I figured I'd find her, mate with her, then take her home to meet Mama so we could live happily ever after. I was stunned by her obvious reluctance to be with me despite the strong attraction simmering between us.

I slid my palm down Dianne's arm and wrapped my fingers around hers. I took it as a victory when she did not pull away from me. Instead, she stared at our joined fingers thoughtfully.

"Look Elijah, I'm sorry you came all this way, but I really didn't mean to call you," she started, still staring down. "I honestly didn't know that I'd inherited anything from the succubus side of my family. You seem like a nice guy, but I don't have the time nor the desire for a mate right now. The fact is, I like my life exactly the way it is."

My heart pinched at her words, but her refusal to meet my gaze told me that she wasn't fully convinced either. Maybe she hadn't called me to her consciously, but some part of her wanted me here. I just needed to help her get in touch with her succubus side. The succubus would help her get past her human resistance.

Releasing her hand, I wrapped my hands around her waist and lifted her off the couch, swinging her around until she was sitting on my lap, knees on either side of my legs. Her skirt slid high on her thighs, exposing silky pale skin.

Dianne blinked, as if unsure what had just happened, and opened her mouth, no doubt to let me have it.

I was faster.

My hand cupped the back of her head, holding her still, and I leaned forward to capture her lips. Dianne made a little gasping noise against my mouth, but she didn't punch me in the junk, so I took that as a good sign, especially since it was within arm's length.

Sweeping my tongue into her mouth, I tangled my tongue with hers and began exploring her mouth. Her breath tasted sweet, probably from the fruity cocktail she'd been drinking when I found her at the bar earlier.

I knew the minute her resistance faded. She sighed again, and then my mate's small hands came to my shoulders, gripping the fabric of my shirt. She became more active, kissing me back with much enthusiasm. I slid my hands down to her ass, pulling her closer to me, and she ground her pelvis against my hardened cock.

It wasn't like I was a virgin – as a professional football player I often had women throwing themselves at me, and I sometimes took what they offered – but with my mate, everything was totally different. Everything was brighter somehow, and more intense. I felt like I could kiss her all day and never get tired of the taste of her sweet lips.

I was a pretty simple guy, calm and collected most of the time, but with Dianne in my arms, our mouths fused together, I felt a sense of calm and peace that I didn't even know was lacking.

When we were out of breath, I pulled back a bit, nipping along her jaw and down the side of her neck. She dropped her head to the side, giving me better access, her breath coming in short bursts as she continued grinding against me.

"Do you need me to get you off, little mate?" I whispered against her skin. I felt gratified by how quickly I'd been able to bring her to the edge.

"Yes." Her voice was so low that I almost couldn't hear her.

I kissed her again, but kept my hands busy, sliding her skirt up higher until my fingers met the damp fabric at the junction of her legs. I slid one finger up and down the fabric a few times, then pushed it aside. My finger met soft, dripping flesh. I moved in between her pussy lips, stroking through her moisture with a gentle touch.

Breaking the kiss, I inserted my pointer finger into her tight channel and rotated my arm so I could press the heel of my palm against her clit. I pumped in and out while she ground against my hand, getting the pressure she needed to come apart with a loud gasp.

"Ahh!"

She was convulsing in pleasure, thrashing around enough that I had to grip her hip with my other hand to keep her from flying off my lap.

I stared at her beautiful face. Her eyes were closed, lips parted, cheeks flushed, and head tilted to the side while she succumbed to her release. I sent up a small prayer to all the gods in the heavens that things would work out between us so I could see that face every day for the rest of my life.

Dianne

I fell against Elijah's chest, completely wrung out from my orgasm. Gently he removed his soaked finger from inside my pussy.

"Delicious," he whispered.

I looked up and saw him sucking my essence off his finger. Goddess help me, it was one of the most erotic things I'd ever seen. My mind raced as I realized I'd just had the fastest and most intense orgasm of my life at the hand of the guy my succubus side called to us.

That couldn't be a coincidence.

I didn't doubt that Elijah was my fated mate. I would have known it the minute I saw him, even without my long-dormant demon side coming awake. There was just this...sense I had when I first saw him. I couldn't really describe it other than to say if felt like I'd found something important that I didn't even know was missing.

But damned if that idea didn't scare the shit out of me. I'd lived my entire life on my own, taking care of myself, depending only on me, ever since I was very young. The idea of having someone else depend on me – or me depending on them – scared me shitless.

Depending on people always led to heartbreak. I knew this from personal experience.

Feeling a sense of rising panic, I shifted on Elijah's lap. I needed some space, needed to get away from this giant so I could think clearly.

"You are going to run away now, aren't you, little mate?"

Elijah's voice grumbled in his chest, beneath my cheek, and I felt the sudden need to comfort him. I was not a person who comforted people, ask any of my friends. I was the one you came to for tough love, not commiseration. Yet I rubbed my hand on his chest, soothing him.

"Yeah, I need to go," I acknowledged, shifting on his lap to meet his eyes.

When I moved, his enormous cock twitched beneath me. Holy crap, how big was that thing? My eyes lowered, studying the outline in his pants.

"Do you, um, want me to take care of that for you?" I asked, nodding toward his bulge.

Elijah slid one thick finger beneath my chin, forcing me to meet his gaze.

"As appealing as that is, little mate, I can see that you are still unsettled and require some time to process your thoughts."

Grabbing my waist, he shifted me over to sit on the couch again, then pressed his hand against his erection with a slight wince. It had to be uncomfortable for him.

Elijah took a deep breath and blew it out slowly before facing me again.

"I will walk you out."

I couldn't believe he was letting me go, after his caveman tactics earlier. Maybe once he'd gotten closer to me, he wasn't as interested as he was before. Maybe he didn't really find me attractive. Was that why he didn't want a blow job? I mean, what guy refused a blow job?

"You look sad now, little mate, why is that?"

I was surprised at his perceptiveness.

"Um, what we did just now, that was okay for you?"

I felt a flash of irritation at the insecure tone in my voice. That was not like me.

"I mean, I'm just surprised you're okay with me leaving after you dragged me here over your shoulder and all. And without getting any relief for yourself."

My eyes returned once again to his crotch, as if pulled by a magnet.

Lumbering to his feet, Elijah exhaled strongly again, and pulled me up to stand next to him. He looked down at me with a tender look, one palm coming to cup my cheek, and I couldn't help but lean into his gentle touch.

"I'm trying to give you the space you require," he said seriously. "If you no longer want space, I will gladly carry you into my bedroom and fuck you for the rest of the night until we are completely imprinted on each other as mates."

My eyes widened at his coarse language. My already soaked panties took another shot of moisture. Shoving aside the visual that Elijah's words brought to mind, I stepped away from him. Something deep inside me immediately mourned the loss.

"You will see me again tomorrow," Elijah stated.

My hackles were up again. It was easier to focus on my irritation than the more complicated feelings that Elijah brought out in me.

"What did I tell you about bossing me around, you big oaf?"

"My apologies, little mate. Please, may I see you tomorrow?"

"I have to work tomorrow."

"What time do you get off work?"

"Five, if there's not an emergency."

"I will see you then."

He leaned forward and pressed a soft kiss to my forehead.

"I will look forward to seeing you again in person. In the meantime, I will see you in my dreams."

Leaving his Airbnb, I stalked back to the bar to grab my car, then called my mother the minute the Bluetooth connected.

"Mom?"

To my surprise, she picked up right away, sounding sober. Mom loved the psychedelic mushrooms as well as her gin.

"Dianne dear, how are you? It's been a while."

It had been a while because my mother was flighty as hell – and that was the kindest way I could put it. I knew she loved me, but she was forever going off on a quest or falling in love with a new man or getting lost in a field of poppies or some damn thing. It made her a shitty parent. She often forgot things like birthdays, holidays, and coming home to the eight year old daughter she'd left home alone with an empty refrigerator.

"I need to know about your succubus."

My mother's laugh tinkled over the speakers. "Oh, it's finally happened, hasn't it? I was starting to think it never would."

"What are you talking about?"

"Your inner demon has risen, hasn't she? You've found your mate. Or at least someone you really like."

"I guess? How did you know that?"

"You were never interested in your succubus side before. Your grandmother and I were worried you were a latent or something," Mom explained. "Usually a succubus is calling for her first soulmate by the time she's in her early twenties."

"First soulmate?"

"Our kind can have several soulmates."

"I'm pretty sure that's the opposite of the definition of a soulmate."

"Soulmate, playmate, whatever. We can all have many loves throughout our lives."

"But what about the succubus? Will it start talking in my head or something?"

"Don't be ridiculous, dear. You're not a shifter." She said this with disdain. "Your succubus side will be more like an impression, a sense of what you should do. Unless you are sleeping of course. They often talk very clearly in your dreams."

"I don't understand."

"I'm sorry, but I have to go, dear. I have a date with a hot young fae and he will be here any minute. But I'd love to meet your man sometime soon if we wind up in the same place."

She hung up without saying goodbye. I wished my grandmother was still alive, maybe she could have shed some light on my situation. I guess I'd have to figure this whole mate thing out on my own.

I turned my car towards the Rosewater Emporium. Maybe I could find something at the town's supernatural store. Cami, who was Pepper and Meri's oldest sister, was working behind the desk, a giant baby bump pressing against the counter. The pretty witch had been running the family store as long as I'd been in Greysden and had recently mated with a local wolf.

"Oh hey Dianne," she greeted me. "I thought you'd be with your giant mate – if you were outside at all."

I looked at her in surprise. "Good lord, I just met the guy a couple of hours ago. You people in Greysden really have gossip down to a science, don't you?"

Cami laughed. "You know it. How can I help you?"

"I'm looking for a book about succubus relationships," I said. "I'm trying to figure out why after years of my inner demon being latent, she's suddenly reared her head and called herself a mate."

"I know just the thing."

Elijah

After Dianne left I ordered a couple of large pizzas and watched ESPN until I was sleepy enough to go to bed. It had killed me to let Dianne go, but I knew she needed a little time to adjust to what was happening between us. That didn't keep me from mourning her absence.

My night was filled with dreams of Dianne. I woke up early, as was my custom, and went for a short ten-mile run.

I'd already fallen in love with the little town Dianne lived in. The streets were bustling with people despite the early hour, and as I ran through downtown on my way to the woods, I noted all the flowers in pots and cute little springtime decorations in the windows. Everyone I passed was friendly, waving as I ran by like I was an old friend.

After my ten-miler, I returned to my rental and downed a protein drink before doing an hour of bodyweight exercises, alternating between squats, push-ups, army crawls, and sit-ups. By the time I got to my stretching routine, my muscles were tingling with exertion. I took a shower before heading back out to grab some food at the Xenakis Diner on Main Street. I didn't have any food in my rental, and I was starving after my workout.

The Xenakis Diner was like every small town diner I'd ever visited: clean, a little bit dated, and filled with people who eyed a stranger with avid curiosity. I was greeted by an older Greek man who smelled like a shifter, but I couldn't identify his species. Probably one of the smaller shifters, I thought.

"Hello, welcome to Xenakis Diner," he greeted me from somewhere near my abs. "My, you're a big fella, please pick any table that fits you."

Bypassing the booths, I grabbed a seat at a table in the center. The little shifter came over with a coffee pot and a menu.

"I am Mr. Xenakis, the owner," he said in a friendly voice. "I haven't seen you here before, I don't believe."

"My name is Elijah," I told him, doing a quick scan of the menu. "This is my first visit to Greysden."

"What brings you to our fine town?" he asked. I loved the way people in small towns didn't hesitate to get up in your business.

"I came here to claim my mate."

His face brightened. "Of course, you are the man who carried Dianne out of Murphy's Bar last night. I'm surprised you're here alone after finding your mate. When I was first with my mate, I couldn't bear to be away from her for more than a few minutes."

I knew what he was hinting at: Dianne and I should be fucking each other's brains out right now. I couldn't say I disagreed with the sentiment.

"Dianne had to work today," I said shortly. "I'll take three lumberjack platters with an order of pancakes please."

"Three lumberjack platters?" His eyes widened comically at my large order. "Is someone joining you?"

I patted my flat stomach. "No. It takes a lot of calories to maintain this body."

"Okay, three lumberjacks and an order of pancakes coming right up. Would you like anything else with that?"

Under his breath he mumbled, *"A side of beef maybe?"*

"I'll take a pitcher of orange juice with my coffee, thank you."

He returned less than fifteen minutes later with a tray laden with three huge platters of breakfast foods, a stack of pancakes, and a pitcher filled to the brim with orange juice. I tucked into my food, happy to find that everything was delicious.

After eating my breakfast I headed to the occult store I'd seen on my run, the Rosewater Emporium. I wanted to learn more about Dianne's succubus side so I could figure out how to work things out with her.

I was greeted by a lovely pregnant woman a few years younger than me. She had long brown hair and was dressed in a flowy skirt and a tunic, with sandals on her feet. She didn't smell like a shifter, and based on the little thread of magic in her aura, I guessed that she was probably a witch. She was a beautiful woman, but I only had eyes for my mate now.

"Welcome to Rosewater Emporium, I'm Cami. How may I help you today?"

"I'm looking for a book about relationships, specifically, a relationship with a succubus. Or any information on being a latent succubus, if you have something like that."

"Well, that's a popular topic here lately, Elijah. Come this way and I'll show you what I have."

"How did you know my name?" I asked curiously as she led me through the shelves overflowing with books.

"You're the only Nephilim in town who wants to mate a succubus who just came into her powers," she explained. "At least as far as I know. Plus it's a small town and news travels fast. My sisters Pepper and Meri were with Dianne when you found her at Murphy's last night."

Cami pulled a book off the shelf, handing it to me. "I think this will be super helpful."

Another book followed. "This one too."

"Great, thanks Cami. I appreciate the help."

I spent the rest of the day reading about the nature of the succubus type of demon, including their mating habits. Nothing in the book explained Dianne's reluctance to be with me though. That had to be about something else.

At four fifty-five I walked into the Rutherford Industries office intent on finding my little mate. I could sense Dianne's presence as soon as I opened the door, so I bypassed the startled receptionist and just headed straight for her office.

Dianne was seated at her desk, the wolf from last night sitting in a chair across from her.

"It's time to go," I said in greeting.

My mate's eyes immediately sparked with anger.

"You can't just barge in here and interrupt me, Elijah," she snapped. "I'm working here. Also, a greeting would be nice before you start ordering me around!"

It seemed that I had made yet another misstep with my mate. I should really call my mama for some advice on this situation.

Preston stood up. "We're done here anyway, why don't you take off now, Dianne? I know you kids have a lot to talk about."

"Whose side are you on, Preston?" she snipped.

"I'm on the side of true love," he said, giving her a goofy smile. "You helped me with Meri, now I'll help you work things out with your own mate. I'll see you tomorrow."

I tipped my chin at him as he left the office, still smiling.

Dianne opened a drawer and pulled out her purse, slinging it across her chest. When she looked at me again, she still seemed irritated.

"We had plans tonight, remember?" I asked her.

"I do, but you need to learn boundaries, Elijah."

"Okay," I agreed. I'd do whatever I needed to do to make my mate happy. I strode across the room and picked her up bride style. "Let's go."

She nailed me in the chest with one of her elbows.

"This is not good boundaries," she protested. "Now put me down, you big oaf."

"I like carrying you." I did, too. It made me feel strong and protective.

"Well I don't like it at all," she grumbled, but the rapidly beating pulse in her throat and the hardening of her nipples told another story.

"Are you planning to carry me all the way home, genius?" she asked. "Because my car is here in the parking lot."

Reluctantly I put her back on her feet. "We will go out to dinner. I will court you as part of our mating ritual."

I'd read about succubus mating rituals in the book I'd picked up today, so I was sure this plan would work.

"Are you asking me or telling me?" she asked.

"Asking."

She huffed out a breath. "Fine, but I'd really like to change first and feed Mr. Fluffers."

"I will follow you there."

She rolled her eyes, then stomped over to a tiny little Toyota. It was much too small and fragile of a vehicle to keep my little mate safe, and I resolved to procure her new transportation in the morning. I followed her home in my custom-made SUV, watching her carefully.

Dianne's place was a cute little bungalow on a corner lot, surrounded by a high fence. She pulled into her driveway, and I parked my truck on the street in front of her house.

"I just need a few minutes," she said as I met her on the walkway. "You might as well come in."

She seemed less than enthused, but I tried not to let it bother me. I just needed to spend more time with her, then she would realize that I was as perfect for her as she was for me.

Dianne opened the door, and I followed her into the house. The next thing I knew, I was under attack.

Dianne

"Mr. Fluffers! Bad boy!"

My normally sweet cat had gone bonkers. The minute we stepped into the house he'd launched himself at Elijah, hissing and clawing. He seemed to be everywhere at once as I struggled to pry his claws out of my guest. Finally I got a hold of his scruff and pulled him away, his body vibrating with rage. I hurried over to the laundry room where I kept the litter box and closed him inside.

"You're grounded, Mr. Fluffers," I scolded through the door. "Bad boy!"

When I turned around, Elijah was right behind me. For a big guy, he walked very quietly. His tee shirt was ripped in several places, and he had a long bloody scratch on his forearm.

"Oh no, you're hurt. I'm so sorry."

I grabbed his wrist, ignoring the buzzing sensation that always started when we touched, and tugged him into the kitchen.

"Sit down, I'll get the first aid kit."

I rushed into the bathroom and returned with the first aid kit in hand. Elijah looked the tiniest bit freaked out.

"Why does your cat hate me? I didn't even do anything to it."

He paused.

"Maybe he did not understand that my talk of eating him was a joke?"

"I have no idea what got into him. He's never done anything like that before," I said, leaning down to look at his arm more closely. The scratch was long and angry looking.

"This is going to sting," I warned as I pulled out the antiseptic.

Elijah was stoic as I cleaned the wound and smeared it with antibiotic cream. I glanced at his shredded shirt.

"Did he scratch your chest too?"

"Yes."

"I'd better take a look." I dropped to my knees between his legs, ignoring the suggestive nature of my position. "Take off your shirt."

He pulled off his shirt, revealing a series of scratches that I cleaned and treated. Elijah didn't so much as wince, even though I knew the antiseptic on all those scratches had to sting.

When I was done, I couldn't resist putting my hands on his thighs. They were enormous, enough that my hands looked tiny in comparison. I looked up at Elijah from under my lashes.

"I would offer you another shirt, but I'm certain I don't have anything big enough to fit you here."

"It's okay," he said, reaching for his discarded shirt. "I will just put this one back on."

We both looked at his tattered shirt, flashes of his phenomenal chest visible beneath the rips.

"You can't go out in public like that. Maybe we should get delivery and eat here instead?" I suggested.

"That sounds good."

For a guy who'd just been assaulted by a cat, all of a sudden he seemed very pleased with himself.

"There's a decent Italian place that delivers," I said, plucking the menu from a drawer. "Why don't you pick out what you want while I change out of my work clothes? I'll be right back."

Once in my bedroom, I changed into worn yoga pants and an ancient pink sweatshirt. It didn't take a psychologist to figure out that I was trying to make myself less attractive. And Elijah knew it too, if the smirk he shot me when he saw my outfit was anything to go by. But thankfully he didn't comment.

"The food will be here in thirty minutes," he said.

"You ordered for me? You didn't ask me what I wanted." This guy's pushiness was really annoying me.

"I ordered one of everything, so whatever you want, we will have it here."

"One of everything?" I picked up the menu and scanned the list. "That's like twelve dishes."

"I am hungry."

I just stared at him with my mouth open, until he slid one finger beneath my chin and pushed it closed again.

"Keep your mouth open like that, little mate, and I will think of other uses for it."

I turned on my heel and stalked to the refrigerator, muttering under my breath. "Damn succubus, you stay silent for thirty-eight years and when you finally wake up, *this* is who you call for me?"

"Most people like me," Elijah called back.

I grabbed a beer, twisting off the cap and taking a long pull of the cold and bitter liquid while leaning my hip against the sink.

Elijah stalked towards me, a look of intent on his face. He was so freaking big that I had to crane my neck to look at him, which I did not appreciate. I was pretty tall for a woman, and I wasn't used to feeling short.

He grabbed the beer from my hand, helping himself to a long drink, then set it down behind him.

"What are you doing?" I tried, and failed, to keep the nervousness out of my tone.

He backed me up to the counter, then lifted me up without a word. When I was seated on the countertop, I popped my knees together tight to keep him from moving closer. But Elijah just smirked again and leaned over my legs, arms coming to the counter on either side of me. With the cabinet behind me, I felt trapped.

"This is what I'm doing," he whispered before his mouth crashed against mine.

I raised my hands to his chest, intending to push him away, but as soon as our lips touched, my entire body felt electrified. Any thought of pushing him away went right out of my head. Instead, my hands rose to his broad shoulders, dragging him closer while his tongue plundered my mouth.

Damn this man was a great kisser. I'd never been kissed with this much finesse, this much passion. I'd never become this aroused just from making out.

I wanted him. I wanted him badly. But I knew if I gave in, if we had sex, the mate bond would activate, and I'd be tied forever to a man I'd only known for two days.

He's already ruined you for other men, and you haven't even had full-on sex with him yet, a voice deep inside me taunted.

As I'd read in the book that Cami had recommended to me last night, demons didn't have the same kind of mate bonds as shifters. We couldn't read each other's emotions and locate each other through the bond like the shifters did. But if you met your soulmate and consummated the relationship, there would be a soul bond that grew between you. After that, it would basically be impossible to be with anyone else until one of you died. It was like a mystical marriage.

There were some exceptions to this, but most demons were monogamous just like shifters. At least after they found the right person...

With a huge amount of effort, I pushed against Elijah's shoulders and moved my lips away from his. I couldn't be tied to someone, not now, not ever.

"Stop."

To his credit, he stopped immediately. I shimmied around him and jumped off the counter.

"Did I do something wrong?" he asked.

There was something innocent and endearing about him. It was impossible to dislike the gentle giant, no matter how bossy he was.

"We need to pump the brakes on this, Elijah. I need time to process everything that's happened."

He nodded. "Process. Okay. You may process."

I bit back a sarcastic retort. "Do you want to watch a movie or something? We can eat in the living room when the food comes."

"Sure. I would like to spend more time with you, little mate."

As much as I hated to admit it, Elijah and I had a nice evening together. We wound up watching several episodes of The Office after I realized he'd never seen it.

"There is no football in this show," he told me with a serious tone.

"Well, you've been missing out then," I rejoined.

While we watched the comedy, we ate an enormous amount of Italian food, shared a bottle of wine, and talked. I noticed that as we spent more time together, Elijah's speech pattern got a little less stilted, as if he didn't feel the need to be so careful with me.

Just after nine o'clock, Elijah stood up, rubbing his palms down his thighs.

"I should go back to my temporary residence now, little mate."

I'd half expected him to try to stay over, and I couldn't decide if I was relieved or disappointed that he didn't ask. I walked him to the door, and after laying a chaste kiss on my lips, he stepped out onto the porch.

"Thanks for hanging out," I told him.

"I had fun as well. Now lock the door behind me."

I rolled my eyes at his order.

"See you in my dreams tonight, Dianne."

And damned if he didn't. Because I certainly saw him in mine.

Elijah

I woke up hard as a rail. My night had felt like one long dream starring my mate. In my dream we did everything I longed to do in real life, and knowing that she had the ability to get into my dreams, whether it was conscious or not, the dream confirmed that I was on the right path. My mate's resistance was fading as her desire for me increased.

Just like yesterday, I got up early, worked out for a couple of hours, then had a meal at the Xenakis Diner before spending the afternoon reading and relaxing until it was time to pick up my mate from work. It was a routine I could easily get used to.

I strolled into my mate's office at four fifty-five, once again bypassing the receptionist and going right back to find Dianne. The girl at the desk just sighed at me in irritation as I stalked past her.

My mate was at her desk, staring intently at something on her computer screen. Her hair was twisted up in a knot that was secured with a pencil, and her nose was scrunched, the way it did when she was confused or deep in thought, causing the reading glasses on her face to tilt. Looking at her made my heart swell with emotion.

Not wanting to interrupt her, I stood quietly in the doorway until Dianne looked up. She jumped, pressing a hand against her sternum.

"Holy crap Elijah! You scared me."

"It is time to leave," I said, moving into the office.

"We didn't have plans."

"We are mates. Every night we will have plans now."

She shot out of her chair like it was on fire. "You don't get to tell me how to spend my free time!"

I sighed deeply and dropped into the chair across from her desk. It creaked alarmingly under my weight. Steepling my fingers together, I met her gaze and channeled the information I'd read in the books about supernatural mating.

"When you find your mate, it's natural to want to spend as much time with that person as possible, especially in the beginning."

"It's true." A voice came from the doorway. I turned to see her boss Preston standing there. "I remember when Meri and I first got together I couldn't wait to get off work so I could spend time with her."

"I remember when you and Meri got together you thought she was too young and too weird for you, and you wanted nothing to do with having a mate," Dianne retorted.

He gave her a charming smile.

"See? You should learn from my mistakes. One should never question fate. And once I realized how great it was to have a mate, I couldn't get enough of her."

"Yeah, we all know. We heard you banging in your office at lunch yesterday."

Preston laughed. "You kids have fun. I'll see you in the morning for our conference call with Munich."

Dianne powered down her computer, then retrieved her bag from her desk drawer.

"I supposed we could go have dinner," she said grudgingly. "Or we—-!" Her words cut off as I picked her up in my arms.

"Damn it Elijah, put me down!"

I walked towards the door with her in my arms. "I like carrying you," I told her, tightening my grip around her. "You are so little and soft."

"Does mental illness run in your family?"

"Not to my knowledge."

Just like yesterday, I carried her out to the parking lot. Setting her down by her car, I said, "I will meet you at your home."

She rolled her eyes – something she seemed to do a lot around me—but got into the car. I followed closely behind her, eager to be there when she saw my surprise.

We arrived at Dianne's house quickly, and she swung her little car into the driveway, nearly rear-ending the shiny black Hummer I'd left there for her. It was encased in a thick red ribbon, a giant bow affixed to the hood. She backed out onto the street, parking by the curb, then stalked to my car as I pulled up behind her.

"What the hell is that?"

"What?" I asked, striving for an innocent face.

She took a deep breath. "Did you have anything to do with that huge black monstrosity in my driveway?"

"It's not a monstrosity," I defended. "It is a safer vehicle for you to drive."

"My Camry is perfectly safe – and paid for, I might add."

"It's basically a tin can. If someone hits you, you will be hurt. And the Hummer is also paid for."

"You are not giving me a damn car! That's way too expensive of a gift."

"Don't worry." I patted her arm. "I'm extremely rich. I have millions of dollars in the bank. I can give you anything that you desire."

She threw up her hands and stomped up to her porch, her high heeled shoes striking the wood with intensity. When she opened the door, I tossed in a little catnip mouse I'd picked up as a peace offering for Mr. Fluffers. He stood in the entryway, hissing at it suspiciously. I went to plan B.

"Here you go Mr. Fluffers, I brought you some tuna treats." I pulled a bag of treats out of my pocket and shook it. The feline looked at me with interest. He had long gray hair and blue eyes, a very attractive example of his species.

Mr. Fluffers walked over and rubbed himself on my leg. I squatted down and fed him some treats from my hand. When he'd eaten his fill, he picked up his catnip mouse and disappeared down the hallway, his tail held high.

I was relieved that I had won over my mate's feline and mentally thanked my mama for her suggestions to help. I'd had a long conversation with her earlier today about how to best woo my mate.

Dianne watched the entire scene with a bemused look on her face. "I see you're charming my little buddy there."

I pushed to my feet. "I hope to charm you someday the same way."

Her face clouded over. "Look Elijah. It's not that I don't like you. I do. It's not that I'm not attracted to you. Obviously, I am. It's just that I've never wanted a mate. Or a husband, or any kind of life partner. I'm perfectly content being on my own."

Her face looked sad, a shadow of pain in her eyes.

"Did someone hurt you?" I asked, clenching my fists. If someone hurt her, I would kill them. Slowly.

She shook her head. "No. I've...wait, let's not have this conversation in the hallway."

She gestured to the couch. I was pleased when she sat next to me, turning her body to face me as we talked.

"I grew up in a situation that was...not good."

She looked down at her hands, picking at a cuticle. I pulled the hand into mine, engulfing her much smaller hand.

"Growing up the way I did, it taught me that it's better not to rely on anyone else. Other people just let you down, even if they don't mean to do it. It taught me to avoid any serious entanglements."

"So that means that you have never been married, correct?"

She shook her head, looking confused by my question.

"Have you ever lived with a man? Or a female romantic partner?"

She rolled her lips inward like she was trying not to smile. "No."

"How many men have you dated seriously?" I asked, hoping I could get a list.

I would find every one of them and make them sorry they were ever with my mate. Yes, I knew I was being a total caveman, yet I couldn't help it.

"I've never dated anyone for more than a few months," she admitted. "I cut them loose when they start to get serious."

"You are, what, forty years old?"

Her jaw dropped, a look of shocked horror coming to her face. I had a sudden flash of Mama advising us to never ask a woman her age or her weight. Clearly I messed up again.

"Oh my God! Do you think I look like I'm forty?"

The tone of her voice conveyed that she believed I'd called her an old hag.

"No, no," I rushed to answer. "You look young and beautiful. I was merely guessing that you are close to my own age."

"I'm only thirty-eight," she sniffed. "Until next month," she added quietly.

"I am sorry, little mate, you do not look a day over thirty-five."

She shook her head like I was being ridiculous, but her expression softened.

"I am forty years old and like you, I have never married, never lived with anyone, never dated anyone for longer than a few months. And do you know why, Dianne?"

"Because you were an NFL football player who could have a new woman every night of the week?"

I shook my head.

"It was because whenever I was with another woman, I knew instinctively she wasn't you."

"You didn't even know me until a couple of days ago."

I pressed my hand against my chest. "In my heart, I always knew you."

Dianne

I had to give it to Elijah, he was a sweet talker. I was finding it harder and harder to remember why I was resisting him.

Staring deep into his eyes, I moved closer. He sat completely still, letting me take the lead, which made me bolder. I wrapped one hand around the back of his thick neck, drawing his face down towards me, and pressed my lips against his.

We were both totally still for several seconds, our breaths mingling as our lips pressed together. Then I bit his lower lip, hard enough for him to make a little noise of surprise, and I deepened the kiss, sliding my tongue roughly against his. Shifting up to my knees, I moved closer to him, balancing one hand on his shoulder while the other continued to squeeze the back of his neck.

Elijah held himself back for several minutes – practically vibrating with the effort to be still—before his hands finally clamped down on my hips. I thought he was going to pull me onto his lap, but instead he shifted me backwards, maneuvering me until I was laying flat on my back on the cushions. He shifted over me, balancing his weight on his arms. He slid one leg between mine, the other on the outer edge of the couch. The hard bulge of his erection pressed against my thigh.

After we kissed for several long moments, he broke away and moved down a bit so he could shove my shirt up to my armpits, revealing my plain satin bra. He found my nipple, mouthing it through the fabric, the sensation traveling straight down to my core. I moaned softly, my hands reaching above me to hold onto the arm of the couch.

Elijah shifted again, intending to access the other breast I assume, and somehow rolled himself right off my couch. He landed partly on the coffee table, which buckled under his weight. Seven feet and probably three hundred pounds of muscle was just too much for the rickety coffee table that had graced my living room since I was fresh out of college. The cracking of the wood filled the room, followed by Elijah's grunt of pain.

I sat up, seeing him laying on top of the splintered remains of my coffee table.

"Crap! Are you okay, Elijah?"

"Why do I get injured every time I visit your house?" he asked ruefully.

I hopped off the couch and reached out a hand to help him up. He moved to his feet with the grace of the athlete that he was, brushing off splinters of wood from the back of his body.

"Turn around, let me see if you hurt yourself."

I lifted his shirt, examining the muscled expanse of his back. He shivered when I ran my hands over his skin, checking for any injuries. His skin was smooth and unblemished.

"I don't think you have any splinters. Your shirt protected you from the worst of it."

I met his dark eyes and made a decision. I was tired of denying myself – denying us both – of what we really wanted.

"Let's go to my bedroom where it's safer for you."

"Are you saying what I think you're saying, little mate?" he asked, his voice suddenly rough. His eyes darkened, turning almost black.

"Yes."

He stepped closer and I held up a hand to stop him.

"This doesn't mean anything."

I didn't believe that any more than he did. He reached out, tucking a strand of hair behind my ears.

"It means everything," he said firmly.

"Okay, then you need to understand that I can't make you any promises, not right now," I said, trying to make my voice more convincing than I felt inside. "I'm still not sure that I want a mate. All I know is that I want you more than I've ever wanted anyone in my life – and I can't wait to have you."

Before I took my next breath I was hanging over Elijah's shoulder again, just like I was the first night we met.

"Damn it! Stop doing that!" I shouted, pounding on his back.

The effort was half-hearted though. Part of me was thrilled at the easy way he carried me around like I was one of those tiny petite girls. And part of me just liked being eye level with that fantastic ass.

Elijah headed down the hallway, finding my bedroom, then kicked the door closed behind us. Slowly, gently, he slid me down his body until I was on my feet again. I realized that somewhere along the way I'd lost my high heeled shoes, making me even shorter than him.

Feeling bold, I reached for his shirt, slowly opening the buttons one by one, revealing that sculpted chest that I'd seen yesterday. I'd been focused on treating his scratches of course, but I hadn't missed the muscles or that lovely little happy trail that peeked out above his waistband. He looked better than any of the guys you'd see on the cover of a romance novel or a men's fitness magazine.

Elijah stood still, letting me take the lead again. I knew instinctively he wanted to make sure I felt safe. Like I had a choice. I loved that about him. And maybe that wasn't the only thing I loved about him...

My hands grazed his stomach as I reached for his belt, and Elijah hissed out a breath. I looked up at him, giving him a small smile, then undid his pants. The sound of his zipper was loud in the quiet of the room. I pushed his pants off his hips, letting them fall towards his ankles, and my eyes widened as I glimpsed the enormous bulge in his boxers.

If I'd had any doubt about whether every part of him was giant, those doubts were baseless. My mate was definitely proportional.

I cupped him through his boxers, giving him a little squeeze. That seemed to spur him to action. He pulled my shirt over my head with an urgency that made me feel powerful, and practically ripped off my bra. My heavy breasts jiggled as they were released from their confines.

I resisted the urge to suck in my soft stomach. If we were going to be together, he needed to see me for who I really was, tummy rolls and all.

"You're so beautiful, little mate. Better than I even dreamed of." He cupped my breasts in his large hands, his expression almost reverent.

I reached behind me to unzip the skirt I'd worn to work, pushing it down. Elijah dropped to his knees, helping me step out of my skirt, then peppering little kisses around my belly button. It was sweet and weirdly arousing. That close to my core, he had to be able to smell exactly how arousing I found it.

When Elijah lowered his head and grasped the waistband of my panties between his teeth I almost passed out from excitement. Watching me through his thick lashes, he dragged my panties down to my knees with his teeth, his lips brushing against my sensitive skin.

By the time he reached my knees, I was shaking with desire. He finished removing them with his large hands, then leaned back, his eyes hungrily devouring the sight of me bare before him. My pussy was dripping wet.

Without a word, he spread my lower lips apart with his fingers and stroked inside me with his tongue. I let out a soft, startled cry unlike any sound I'd made in my life. He licked me again, deeper, and my knees nearly buckled. I grabbed a handful of his thick hair, pulling his head up.

"If you're going to keep doing that, I'd better lay down before my knees give out," I panted.

He surged up in response, reaching for me. I shook my head in warning.

"I can make it to the bed myself. How about you focus on taking off your boxers –," my eyes raked over his half naked body, "—and your socks."

I plopped my ass onto the bed, shamelessly watching as he shoved his boxers down, revealing an ass that I suddenly wanted to sink my teeth into. For the record, I'd never bitten anyone's ass in my life. He was just so...edible.

Maybe I was making a mistake. Maybe I'd regret sleeping with Elijah. But somehow this all felt so right that I couldn't deny my feelings for him anymore. I was falling for this gentle giant. And I wanted him inside me more than anything in the world.

Assuming he could fit.

Elijah

I turned to face the bed and Dianne's eyes widened. I got that a lot. After all, I was a giant guy, and every part of me was proportional. Not to brag, but I had a very big dick.

My mate looked absolutely delicious sitting there, totally naked. She was curvy and soft and prefect for me. I couldn't decide whether to bury my face between her thighs or bury my cock deep inside her pussy.

"I have an IUD," she whispered. "And I haven't had sex in over a year, so I'm safe – if you are."

My heartbeat sped up at the idea of taking my mate without the barrier of latex between us. I'd never gone without protection before, and I appreciated the trust she was placing in me.

"We get yearly physicals at work, including an STD screen," I told her. "It's been nearly that long for me too."

She looked surprised by my recent dry spell, so I added, "At some point, I got sick of being with anyone who wasn't my mate."

Her face softened. "Come over here, honey."

My heart swelled at the endearment. I reached her in two steps. She settled on her back in the middle of the bed, and I moved into a plank position over her, lowering my head to kiss her but keeping all of my weight off of her. Dianne squeezed my ass, trying to bring my hips closer.

"I'm a big girl," she said, dragging her lips away from mine and giving me a hard tug downwards. "You won't break me."

I brought my lower body down slowly, squeezing in between her legs and lining my hips up with hers. Bending my elbows, I lowered myself until we were touching from head to foot, although I still balanced a good amount of my weight on my legs and forearms.

Once I was settled, I couldn't resist returning to the sweetness of her mouth. I kissed her until we were breathless, then lifted my head to stare into her eyes.

"I'm so glad I'm here with you right now," I told her. "You're so fucking beautiful."

She looked startled. Maybe no one had complimented her before, but I would be complimenting her until I took my last breath. Which would happen soon if I didn't get inside her in the near future. But first, I needed to make sure I prepared her for my extra-large cock. I didn't want to hurt my little mate.

I kissed my way down her body until my shoulders were between her legs. Throwing them over my shoulders, I turned my focus towards getting her off. There would be more time later to savor her, but I was hanging on by a thin thread right now. I did not want to embarrass myself by coming early like a teenager.

I slid one finger into her slick channel, pumping in and out while I watched her face to learn what speed and rhythm she liked. Then I added a second and a third finger, pumping in and out of her at a steady pace. Dianne's hips lifted off the bed to meet me with each stroke.

"That feels so good, please, don't stop."

"I'll take care of you, little mate, don't worry."

While I continued fucking her with my fingers, I snaked my other hand up to find her nipple. I circled it with my thumb several times, then pinched it between my fingers and gave it a little tug. Dianne made a moaning noise, and I could tell from the little tremors around my fingers that she was close.

I shifted slightly so I could suck her clit into my mouth while still pumping into her with my fingers. Her breathing was labored, her eyes squeezed shut as she chased her release. I bent my fingers, finding the little patch of tissue that sent her right over the edge.

"Elijah!" she whimpered as she broke apart beneath me.

I glanced up at her flushed face. My mate looked beautiful as she came, both totally relaxed and intense at the same time, a soft smile gracing her lips. I realized that I was grinding my hips against the mattress, pre-cum seeping from the tip of my cock. But I continued stroking Dianne with my fingers until her movements slowed. I removed my fingers as her internal muscles relaxed.

Resting my chin on her lower belly, I asked, "How was that?"

She lifted her head and looked at me like I was crazy. "I just came my brains out, how do you think it was?"

Pure masculine satisfaction filled me as I confirmed that I had pleased my mate. I wasn't a selfish lover – I'd always made sure that the women I was with got their own satisfaction before I took mine – but never in my life had another person's pleasure been so much more important than my own.

"Are you ready for me now, mate?"

"Yes, Elijah, I want you inside me," she gasped. "Please. Make me yours."

I'm pretty sure I'd never heard better news in my life. It was better than the day I got drafted into the NFL. Better than the time my team went to the Super Bowl. We both knew that there was no going back after this – we would be mated.

I spread Dianne's legs wide so I could line my cock up with her entrance. She slid her legs around my waist, tilting her hips to welcome me in. Slowly, slowly I inserted just the tip of my cock. Dianne hissed.

"Damn, you're a big boy."

I couldn't help but laugh. "That's what my mama used to tell me."

"Are you thinking about your mama when you're in bed with me?" she asked teasingly.

"Don't kill my boner," I grumbled, feeding her a few more inches of my cock now that her internal muscles were relaxing. "I've been waiting for this for too damned long."

Dianne raised her head to give me a quick kiss, and I continued pushing inside her until I was fully seated. When our hips met, we both groaned in pleasure.

"I've never felt this full," she sighed.

"Yeah, I get that a lot."

She raised her head again, this time to glare at me.

"Sorry," I grimaced. "It's hard to think straight when I'm trying not to come on the first stroke."

She gave me a sweet smile. "Then move, Elijah. Don't treat me like a delicate flower."

I started moving then, pumping into her slowly at first, then speeding up as we found a rhythm together. Dianne squeezed my shoulders, her short nails digging deep as she held on.

My strokes turned rougher as I purposely rubbed against her clit with every stroke. I wanted her to get off one more time before I took my own release.

"Come for me again, little mate," I ordered.

"What did I tell you about bossing me around?"

"You said it was okay in the bedroom."

"I did not."

I raised one eyebrow, and then she smiled.

"Fine."

It took a few more long, hard strokes before she started trembling beneath me. Her inner muscles squeezed me, her entire body vibrating as the orgasm hit her. Her mouth was open in a silent scream as she broke apart around me.

That was it for me. I pumped into her once. Twice. Three times. A tingling shot down my spine. And then I succumbed to the pleasure, releasing my cum deep inside her with a groan. I'd never even remotely considered getting a woman pregnant before, but as I filled her womb with my seed, I couldn't help but imagine Dianne rounded with my child.

The air seemed to shiver around us, and I felt a jolt deep inside me, followed by a sense of euphoria. The mate bond. Dianne shivered, and I wondered if she felt it too. I rolled to the side and pulled her close to me while we both recovered. She snuggled into my chest, her head resting on my arm.

"Hey Dianne?"

"Yeah?" My mate sounded sleepy.

"How do you feel about having a baby?"

She rolled away and sat straight up, her sleepiness suddenly gone.

"What is wrong with you?" she demanded. "Why would you ask me that now?"

"I was just wondering," I defended myself.

"There are three things you never do when you're having sex with a woman, or when you're still in the post-orgasm glow," she chastised, counting them off on her fingers. "One, say you love them for the first time, two, ask them to marry you, or three, ask them to carry your child."

"I didn't realize these were the rules."

"They are. Everyone knows this."

I stretched my arm out in a silent entreaty to come back to me. She laid back down, and I pulled her into my arms. She rested her head on my chest again, and I tightened my arm around her shoulders.

"So was that a yes?"

Dianne

When I woke up the next morning I was super hot. Did I have a fever or something? Opening my eyes, I realized that I was surrounded by a literal giant.

Elijah's chin was pressed against the top of my head, one beefy arm was slung over my waist with fingers pressed against my upper stomach, and the entire back of my body from shoulders to feet was connected to Elijah.

His breathing was slow and deep behind me, allowing me some time to think. Sleeping with him was probably a big mistake but it had felt so perfect – all three times. My giant had fucked me to the point on insensibility.

I wasn't inexperienced in bed – not by a longshot – but I'd never been so affected by having sex with someone before. I woke up feeling all warm and gooey and affectionate, but I wasn't sure if it was the imprinting of our mate bond or if I was catching feelings for Elijah. Maybe both. Either way, it freaked me out.

Slowly I started to move away from the huge man spooning me from behind. The arm around my waist tightened, keeping me in place.

"Stay," he grumbled.

Why did everything have to sound like an order with this guy? Not that I'd minded last night when he'd ordered me to get on my hands and knees and then pounded into me from behind with his fist wrapped around my hair.

"I have to pee." I could hear the snippiness in my voice. "And I need coffee."

"Coffee is good," he mumbled, rolling to his back and falling asleep again.

I shook my head and headed to the bathroom to take care of my bio needs and brush my teeth. I pulled on some sweats and went into the kitchen to brew up some coffee. For a split second I debated making breakfast, but then I remembered something my mother had told me: if you feed strays they just keep coming back.

It was harsh, but I wasn't sure I wanted him getting any ideas, no matter how incredible the sex had been last night. A few sips of coffee later I realized that my thoughts were uncharitable. I was the one who initiated things last night. I was the one who asked him to stay.

With a deep sigh, I opened the fridge to see what I had in there, coming up empty. I couldn't make breakfast after all. Unless Elijah wanted dry corn flakes.

As if my thoughts called him, Elijah wandered into the kitchen wearing nothing but his boxers. He yawned and scratched his belly, drawing my gaze down to his impressive package.

No, bad Dianne, I chastised myself. *Keep your eyes up.*

"Good morning," he said, his voice rough. "Mind if I get some of that coffee?"

"Help yourself."

He kissed my head as he headed to the coffee pot, propping his hips against the counter to mimic my stance. We both drank our coffee in silence for a few minutes before he spoke again.

"I'm starving."

One thing about hanging out with a giant: he was always starving. I still couldn't believe how much Italian food he'd put away the other night.

"Well, we worked up an appetite last night," I reminded him.

"How about if we go to breakfast?" he asked. "The little shifter who runs the diner makes a great lumberjack platter. Unless you have other plans?"

I opened my mouth to say no.

"That sounds good. Let me change my clothes."

Oops.

Then again, who was I kidding? I kind of liked spending time with him. Even if he did talk about football a lot. I mean, I liked football as well as the next person, but Elijah's obsession with the sport was next level. He'd even mumbled about it in his sleep last night. Although I guessed it made sense, given it was his career.

Elijah insisted that I try out the ginormous Hummer he'd bought for me. I got into the driver's seat, grumbling the whole time about how I didn't want a new car and I wasn't going to accept it. Until I started driving it. Turns out the damned thing drove like a dream. And being up this high, I could see much farther when I drove.

Still, as much as I liked the drive, I couldn't accept an expensive car from this guy. Or any car.

We parked in front of the Xenakis Diner, sliding into a booth alongside the window. The diner was crowded with weekend diners, but Mr. Xenakis hustled over to our table right away. The shifter gave us a big smile.

"Mr. Giant. Back for more lumberjack platters?"

Elijah returned his smile. "Yes please, I will have three, with a bowl of oatmeal and a cup of fruit. Plus coffee and orange juice."

My jaw dropped. "You are eating *three* lumberjack platters?" I asked incredulously.

"They are very good, and a lot of food. What do you want to eat, little mate?"

I ordered a Greek omelet and a cup of coffee, then looked around the diner. I didn't eat out often, but I had been here a few times and liked it. While it was a little dated with décor straight out of the nineteen nineties, it was clean and comfortable. There were rows of booths on two sides and freestanding tables lined up in the center. In the back I could see Mrs. Xenakis working in the kitchen along with a guy I hadn't seen before.

I'd been in Greysden long enough now that most people who lived here at least looked familiar, even if I hadn't officially met them. It was a far cry from New York City, that's for sure. Back there I wouldn't have been able to pick my own neighbors out of a lineup.

Elijah and I chatted about Greysden while we ate our breakfasts, keeping our conversation casual as if by unspoken agreement. Periodically someone would stop to say hi to me, clearly curious about who I was eating with. Mr. Xenakis had just cleared our plates when I heard a loud squeal.

"Elijah! My baby!"

I turned to see a very tall and broad woman racing towards us, two carbon copies of Elijah right behind her. My companion's eyes widened.

"I'm so sorry," he whispered urgently. "Please don't be mad at me. I didn't know she was going to come, I swear."

Mrs. Thomas descended on our table, leaning down to give her son a hug.

"This must be my new daughter," she crowed, giving me a friendly smile as she literally dragged me out of my seat for a hug. She was at least six inches taller than me, well over six feet. As she pulled back, she gave me a once-over.

"Oh good! She's got nice wide hips! That will make all the babies come out so much easier!"

Elijah

My poor little mate looked like she wanted to puke. Her cheeks were pink with embarrassment, making me feel even more protective than I usually did. I tugged her out of my mother's grasp and tucked her into my side, feeling gratified when she snuggled against me.

"Mama! Don't embarrass my mate!"

"Sorry dear, I'm just so excited."

"Dianne, this is my mother Annabelle Thomas, and my brothers Zeke and Adam."

"It's very nice to meet you," Dianne greeted them politely.

"I can't believe Tiny found a mate before us," my brother Zeke said.

"Tiny?" Dianne asked in confusion.

"That's his nickname," my brother Adam explained. I shot him a glare. "Because he's the youngest and the smallest."

"We're identical, nitwit," I growled. "And I'm only an inch shorter than you two. How did you all find me, anyway?"

"Easy. You said you were in Greysden, so once we got here, we just activated our triplet radar."

I gave them a skeptical look.

"We asked people on the street where to find you," Mama clarified. "You're the only giant in town. At least until today."

Dianne started to pull away. "I should go and let you all catch up."

"Don't leave," Mama said. "We came to get to know you."

"Um. Well, I've got to go to work."

I had the strangest feeling that she was lying.

"It's Saturday," I reminded her. She sent me a tiny frown.

"I promised my boss I'd help with a project," she said stubbornly.

"Very well. What time will you be done, little mate?" I asked.

"I don't know. A few hours maybe."

"Okay, we will pick you up when you are finished with your work."

"You don't need to pick me up," she protested. "I have my car. Well, your car. You go have fun with your family."

"It's yours now," I reminded her. "We will all meet you for dinner."

She opened her mouth to protest, but an older woman suddenly appeared at my elbow, seemingly out of nowhere. She had brown hair that fell in waves past her shoulders, liberal strands of grey mixed in, and was wearing a broomstick skirt and a peasant blouse. Magic hummed around her.

"Dianne dear, did I hear you found your mate?"

"Oh hi Mrs. Rosewater, um, I'm not sure yet." She pointed to the group. "This is Elijah, his mother Annabelle Thomas, and his brothers Adam and Zeke. They're all visiting from New York."

"You all have to come to dinner at Rosewater Manor," the woman said with a huge smile. "We're having a barbeque in the yard tonight. Preston and the girls will be there. You can all come between five and six."

"Well, that sounds lovely, we appreciate your invitation," Mama said.

"Dianne will show you how to get there, goodbye now."

The woman took a few steps and then seemed to fade into thin air. I frowned in confusion.

"She's a powerful witch," Dianne explained.

In a town like Greysden, that was enough of an explanation.

"She's Meri, Pepper, and Cami's mom."

I nodded.

"How about we meet at my house at five and we can caravan to the Rosewaters?" she suggested. "It's not that far away, maybe ten minutes."

"That sounds good."

I pulled her close and laid a kiss on her lips that left her looking a little dazed. "See you later, little mate."

I spent the afternoon showing my family around Greysden and the forested areas surrounding the little town. While I was enjoying seeing my family, I had to confess that I was missing my mate terribly.

"You're going to move here, aren't you?" Mama asked as we lounged on a park bench in the park in the town square, taking a break. My brothers were wrestling in the grass like little boys. None of us had lost our desire to be physically active, despite our age.

"Yes," I said. "I will have to figure out my job situation. My mate is very settled here and while she is originally from New York City, she has told me that she likes Greysden much better."

"Your contract with the team is up for renewal anyway, isn't it?" my mother asked.

I nodded. "Yes. They have asked me to return for another three-year contract term, but I've been hesitating to make a commitment. Now I know why."

"What will you do in this tiny little town though?"

"Perhaps I can coach football for the younglings," I mused. "Or maybe offer personal training classes. I do not need money, as I have invested my earnings wisely, but I do like to stay busy."

"Well, your mate is a lovely girl," Mama told me approvingly. "You must get her pregnant immediately though, given her age."

"Give her some time to get used to us being mates first, okay Mama?" I pleaded. "She is already a bit skittish, and I do not wish to scare her off with talk about her age or the size of her hips."

"Understood Tiny. We'll be good."

A few hours later we converged at my mate's house. She was waiting for us on the porch, wearing a pair of pink capri pants with white flats and a white blouse. Her blonde hair was loose around her shoulders, and she'd painted her lips with a shiny pink gloss that I wanted to kiss right off her.

"I think we'll need to take two cars," she said, sidestepping my effort to pull her into my arms. One of my brothers snickered behind me at the obvious snub. I could tell immediately from her demeanor that she had put her walls back up to keep me away.

"I will go with you," I informed her. "My family can follow us in the other vehicle."

She raised one eyebrow but did not call me on my bossiness in front of my family. Dianne headed towards her tiny little car, but I grabbed her elbow and directed her towards the Hummer I'd bought her. She sighed deeply.

"I'm not keeping this car," she said as we pulled out of the driveway with Dianne at the wheel.

"Yes you are. My mate and our children will ride in the safest vehicle possible."

I mentally facepalmed. I'd just told my family not to bring these things up and what had I done? Bring them up.

"Again with the children? Do you have a breeding kink or something?" she said in exasperation. "We don't even know each other well enough to live together, let alone have children together."

"Dianne, you are from the supernatural world, the same as I am. You know that fighting fate is a waste of energy. The mating bond grows strong between us, and I will never be able to be with another woman now." I paused for emphasis. "And you will never be with another man."

Dianne

I had never wanted to strangle someone as much as I wanted to strangle Elijah right now. Given that I'd worked for Preston Rutherford III for so many years, that was saying a lot. I was almost thirty-nine years old, for cripe's sake, I thought the baby ship had sailed.

There was the teensiest, tiniest part of me that was intrigued by the idea of having a baby, then I remembered the size of my mate and his two siblings, and my poor vagina practically sealed itself shut in self-defense.

Plus, shouldn't I have a choice in the matter? Or at least more than a day to think about it? Maybe Elijah was only interested in me as a baby maker. Would he dump me if I refused to have a baby?

Last night had been incredible. I couldn't deny that. I also couldn't deny that I felt the mate bond growing between us. It was hard to describe, kind of like an invisible connection that made me aware of where Elijah was at all times, and a strong instinct that told me to stay as close as possible to him. It had almost hurt to be apart from him this afternoon, which was totally ridiculous.

That desire to stay close, along with the sneaking suspicion that I was already falling in love with him, had triggered my flight response. Well, that and his mother announcing to the diner that I had big hips. That's the kind of thing that was a hit to the ego, no matter how self-confident a person was.

I'd lied earlier when I said I had to go to work. I mean, I did have work to do, but I could have done it Monday. Preston hadn't even been in the office today. It used to be he'd be working seven days a week and whining like a spoiled toddler if I tried to have a weekend off.

But now that he was mated with Meri, his weekends were reserved for his mate, unless she had an event scheduled for her party planning business. Preston's mate had a baffling assortment of part-time jobs, even more baffling because her mate was a billionaire. She certainly didn't need to work anymore now that they were together, but I respected that she did.

"You are angry with me," Elijah said after a few minutes of tense silence.

"I need you to back off," I told him firmly. "You're freaking me out here and you're being way too pushy with all this mate and baby talk. Can you please just...give me some space?"

"Okay." He sounded sad, and I tried not to let it bother me.

When we got to the Rosewater Mansion, Elijah didn't even try to carry me in, which was progress. In a tacit acknowledgement of my request for space, he stayed near his family the entire night, although his eyes never left me.

"What's with you and the big guy?" I looked up as Preston brought me a fresh beer.

He sat down on the bench next to me and gave my shoulder a friendly squeeze, prompting Elijah to make a rumbling noise of warning. My boss and friend bared his fangs and growled in response. I bit my lip to keep from telling both of them that they were idiots.

"He's being super pushy and possessive," I replied softly, cognizant of the number of people here with supernatural hearing.

"We just met a couple of days ago and not only is he already talking about kids and forever, but I'm meeting his mother and she's assessing my ability to birth her grandbabies."

"That's how it is with our kind, you know this."

"Our kind? You're a wolf and I'm a human."

"He's a Nephilim and you're a succubus, neither of you is fully human. I'm guessing that your demon side is on board with Elijah's plan."

"Based on my dreams, sure. She's over the moon. But I just...can't, Preston. I like my independence."

"Independence isn't everything it's cracked up to be," he told me solemnly. "And it's sure not worth making a giant cry."

"I didn't make him cry," I protested.

"He sure looks close."

I followed his eyes to Elijah, who looked downright morose, and sighed deeply as the guilt hit.

"I'll go talk to him."

Grabbing my beer, I went to sit next to my mate. The minute my ass touched the bench next to him, he picked me up and pulled me onto his lap.

"What did I tell you about dragging me around like a rag doll?" I asked in exasperation.

"Sorry," he said immediately, lifting me back to my own chair.

Damned if I didn't miss being on his lap. It was surprisingly comfortable. I put my hand on his arm and leaned in close.

"I don't want to hurt you, Elijah, honestly I don't. But I told you right up front I wasn't interested in having a mate."

For the first time since I'd met him, he looked irritated. For a guy who was normally very easy-going, the change was almost jarring.

"I need to go talk to my brothers."

He stalked away, leaving me gaping after him. The party broke up a short while later, just before ten. After thanking our hosts, I walked out to the cars with Elijah and his family. All of the Nephilim had fit right in with the wacky cast of characters that made up a Rosewater event.

"Your family is very nice," Mrs. Thomas said, sending me a warm smile as we walked out.

"Oh, they're not my family really, they're Preston's."

She cocked her head. "It seems like they've adopted you nonetheless."

Mrs. Thomas turned her attention to her youngest son. "Are you coming back with us, Tiny? Or are you going with your mate?"

It was the first indication I'd had that Elijah's mother had noticed the tension between us. He looked at me, the question clear on his face.

I put a hand on his shoulder and boosted onto my tiptoes, placing a kiss on the edge of his stubbly jaw.

"I'll call you in a few days."

I didn't need to look back to know that Elijah was staring at me like I'd killed his puppy. I could feel it through the bond.

Elijah

"Your mate seems troubled."

My misery must have been palpable, because even my asshole brothers weren't giving me a hard time.

"She says everything is moving too fast for her," I admitted. "Also, it's possible that I made a mistake bringing up children so quickly. She's very human."

"Dianne is an independent woman," Mama noted as we drove towards my Airbnb.

The three of them were staying with me, making me glad that a three-bedroom rental was the only place I could find on such short notice.

"She needs some time to learn that independence doesn't mean that you can't rely on another from time to time. Especially when that other is the one they are fated to be with."

"She does need time," I acknowledged. "It's just that I waited to find my soulmate for forty years. I don't want to waste any time now that I know who she is."

"Did I ever tell you about when your father and I got together?" she asked.

I glanced at my brother's faces in the rearview mirror, noting that they were riveted to the conversation.

"No."

"I had just moved out of my parents' house, and I was renting an apartment on the lower East Side with three of my girlfriends. We were all jammed into the tiniest one-bedroom you've ever seen, but we were enjoying all the delights that Manhattan offers when you are young and single."

I glanced over to see a small smile gracing her beautiful face. We thought she might give up when our father died, but Mama was strong, and she'd rebounded. I was glad she did – we all were.

"I met your father at a bar near my office. He was so big and tall, I knew that he was at least part Nephilim, just like me. Our eyes met over the heads of everyone in the crowd and he stalked over to inform me that I was his mate and that we were leaving."

"What happened?"

"I tossed a dirty martini in his face and told him to leave me alone." She chuckled. "I told him I was too young to have a mate. He looked so confused and hurt. He followed me around like a puppy dog for a solid month, showing up outside of my office, waiting for me on the stoop of my building, but whenever he tried to talk to me I would just ignore him."

"That doesn't sound like you at all, Mama," Zeke said from the backseat.

"I was young and foolish. Like your brother's mate, I didn't want to be tied down. I was afraid that it would mean me losing myself in your father."

I nodded. This sounded very familiar.

"It was only after we spent more time together—after I accepted the bond between us—that I realized having a mate isn't about one person being subsumed by the other. It's about two halves coming together to make something better, a complete whole. It's about one of you filling in the empty spots for the other. It's about an equal partnership. That's what you and your mate both must learn, Elijah."

My mother was right. Dianne wasn't the only one who needed to make some concessions for this to work. I needed to be flexible as well, and I needed to really hear what she was trying to tell me instead of steamrolling over her.

As we pulled up to the rental I put the car in park and turned to give my mother a hug.

"Thanks Mama."

I handed her my key and she opened the car door.

"Come on boys. Your brother needs to go find his mate and fix things with her."

The entire ride over to Dianne's I pondered what to say – although in Greysden, everything was a short trip, so I didn't have much time. I understood her a bit more now that I'd talked to my mama, and I also could see where I had made things worse, but I wasn't sure what to do to fix the damage I'd already created.

I parked on the street in front of my mate's house and sat staring at the dashboard until I heard a knock on the window about five minutes later. Rolling down the tinted window, I saw Dianne standing outside my car with a look of concern on her beautiful face.

Like every time I saw her, my heart swelled with love and happiness. I needed to fix this so we could get to the 'happily ever after' part.

"What are you doing out here, Elijah?"

I noticed that Dianne had changed into sleep shorts and a tee shirt. Her hair was pulled up in a messy bun on top of her head, and she had flip flops on her tiny little feet. She looked cute as hell.

"I'm practicing," I told her honestly.

"Practicing what?"

"What I should say to make you stop being mad at me."

Her lips rolled in like she was amused. "You might as well come in then."

I followed her up the stairs to her house, resisting my natural inclination to carry her. I knew she could walk – obviously – but I just loved the feeling of having her snuggled into my chest. But I understood that being carried wasn't her preference, and resolved to hold myself back when we were in public.

"You want a beer or something?" she asked as we entered the house. Mr. Fluffers raced over to rub himself against my leg before disappearing again when he realized that I didn't have any treats with me. At least he didn't attack me.

"Yes please."

I waited for Dianne in the living room, again ignoring my natural instincts that told me to follow her everywhere she went. She handed me a bottle of beer and sat on the middle cushion of the couch with her own bottle, patting the cushion next to hers.

"Sit."

I sat to her side, turning my body enough to face her. At a loss for words, I started picking at the label of my beer, pulling it away from the icy cold glass.

"Look Elijah, I'm sorry I was bitchy to you. I know I'm sending you mixed messages, sleeping with you and then telling you to leave me alone. The truth is...this whole thing has been discombobulating."

"It's my fault for being too pushy and demanding," I reassured her. "But I will work to do better now that I understand my error."

She laid a hand on my arm, giving it a little squeeze.

"I grew up without a father. As I told you before, my mother was, is...selfish and irresponsible. The kind of person who never thinks of anyone besides herself. When she was around – which wasn't often—it was all about her. I learned early not to ever depend on her, not for food, not to get to school, not to come home at night. I was alone a lot."

My heart squeezed, thinking of my mate as a little girl, all alone in her empty home. I sent a silent prayer to the gods in the heavens thanking them that I'd had not one, but two devoted parents.

"I worked hard to be independent, to create a life where I was safe and secure, and I always promised myself that I'd never let myself rely on anyone else."

I met her sad brown eyes.

"That's the great thing about having a fated mate," I told her. "We can depend on each other, always. When I am weak, you can support me. When you are weak, I can support you. Together we are stronger than we are alone."

"I know you mean that. I know that's how it's supposed to be – I see it with all my friends who have found their mates. But I'm having a hard time believing it."

I placed my hand on top of hers. "Then I will believe it for both of us until you accept it as well."

Dianne put her beer bottle down, then grabbed mine, putting them both on the floor since I'd smashed her coffee table last night. To my shock, she moved to sit crossways on my lap, resting her head on my shoulder and twining her fingers with mine.

"What do you say we try dating for a while and see how it goes?" she whispered. "Let's get to know each other better without the pressure of the mate thing."

"That sounds great."

"When do you have to go back to New York?"

"Never."

"What about your job?"

"My contract is up, and I am technically a free agent. I thought I would move to Greysden to be with you." I phrased it as a question, careful not to be too pushy.

"And do what?"

"I'll find something to keep me occupied," I reassured her. "Until I met you, football was the most important thing in my life. But now you are."

"Really?" she teased. "You like me better than football?"

"Well football is still very important, but now it is second."

"What if things don't work out between us?" she asked. "You'll have uprooted your life for nothing."

"I'll have uprooted my life to try to woo my mate," I corrected. "An acceptable sacrifice. I love you Dianne."

Her mouth opened and I raised my hand to stop her.

"I know you're not there yet, and that's okay, I will wait for you to catch up."

"I don't need time to catch up, Elijah, the truth is...well, I love you too."

My smile was so big it hurt my face.

"But I'm going to need you to be patient with me. I need time to learn to trust you, and to decide whether or not I want to have a baby. If we're going to make this work, we're both going to need to compromise."

"I will gladly compromise with you, little mate, on everything except one thing."

"What's the one thing?" she asked curiously.

"You will drive a safer vehicle."

She huffed out an aggrieved sigh. "Really? That's the one thing you pick?"

"Yes."

"Fine, I'll drive your stupid gas-guzzling car if you do one thing for me."

"What's that?"

"Don't make me sorry that I'm taking a chance on you."

I shifted her until she was straddling my lap, pressing my forehead against hers so I could stare into her eyes and let her see the truth of my words.

"I will never make you sorry, little mate. That is a promise."

Epilogue—Dianne

Four months later...

"Are you ready to go?"

I looked up as Elijah's broad frame filled the doorway of my office. Every day like clockwork he arrived at my office right at five to pick me up.

Escort me from the office, I mean. I had finally broken him of his desire to literally pick me up, at least at work. I had a reputation as a dragon lady to keep up here at the office. I couldn't do that when I was cradled in some giant's arms like an oversized doll.

That didn't keep him from carrying me around in private though. I pretended that I didn't like it, but secretly I kind of did.

"Preston and Duncan and their mates are meeting at Murphy's Bar for happy hour after work. You wanna go?"

"Duncan texted me this update, and I told him that I would be happy to attend," he said.

He and my friends Duncan and Preston had all become good buddies over the last few months, which was good because we all spent a lot of time together.

"Do you need to go home first? I have already fed Mr. Fluffers."

Elijah had basically been living with me the last four months since the barbecue at the Rosewater Mansion. At first he'd kept the Airbnb, but then it seemed silly to spend the money since he spent every night with me.

He still had his condo in New York, but he hadn't been back there once since he'd arrived in Greysden. At some point we'd need to go back there and pack up some of his stuff, even though he planned to keep the condo as an investment.

We never really talked about the two of us living together, but at some point all his stuff had migrated to my house, and I'd made room in the closet and given him a key.

Some might say Elijah had been sneaky about moving in with me, but honestly it was a good approach. I hadn't realized we were moving in together until we'd already been living together, which forestalled any anxiety about it.

Plus my mate wasn't one for long, serious conversations about things like living together. He preferred to show his feelings through his actions.

My place was a little small for the two of us though, and we were already talking about potentially adding an addition onto the back to make an office for him. And by 'office' I think he secretly meant 'man cave'.

Elijah had picked up two part-time jobs since he'd moved to town. During the week he was coaching football at Greysden High School and on Sundays he would be doing commentary for home games for the Denver Broncos. He didn't need an office for either.

Other than his obsessive need to watch every single football game that was on TV ever – sometimes multiple games at once – Elijah was a good person to live with. He was neat and considerate, and he gave me orgasms every day. Really, what more could I ask for?

To my surprise, my mate was also a great cook. Since he wasn't working full-time, he cooked dinner for me every night, a far cry from my meager cooking attempts when I lived alone. It wasn't that I couldn't cook, it was more like I hated to do it. It seemed to give Elijah pleasure though.

I took a deep breath. "Before we go to Murphy's Bar, I need to talk to you about something."

I walked past him and shut my office door, leaning back against the wood as if I needed to keep him from bolting. I don't know why, I was absolutely certain that he was going to be thrilled when he heard my news.

Elijah strode over to me, his palms coming to cup my cheeks. He looked freaked out.

"What is the matter? Have I done something to upset you, little mate?"

"Not really, but clearly you should have played hockey instead of football."

His dark brows lowered over his eyes in confusion. "I do not understand."

"I had a doctor's appointment today. I wanted to her about removing my IUD."

We'd talked about having a baby several times and I'd gradually come around to the idea.

His eyes widened and a huge smile split his face. "Really? You are ready to try to get pregnant?"

"Not exactly."

"What do you mean?"

"It turns out I'm already pregnant. One of your giant sperm made its way past the protection of the IUD."

"You are pregnant?"

"Yes."

"Right now?"

"Yes. About two months along, they think, although I'll know for sure when I get my prenatal scans."

"Is it triplets?" he asked hopefully, one large hand coming to the soft swell of my abdomen.

I squeezed his shoulders in warning.

"If it is, I will kill you with my bare hands. There's no way I'm going to be able to birth three giant babies. But for right now, it's too early to tell."

He grabbed my waist, picking me up and spinning me around.

"I'm going to be a daddy!" he shouted joyfully.

"Put me down, you idiot," I laughed.

"This is the second best day ever."

"What was the first?" I asked curiously.

"The day I met you."

"You're a doofus, but I love you Elijah."

"I love you too. Now let's go tell our friends the news and drink a toast to my incredible virility."

***

If you liked this book please leave a review and let me know! You can read the story of how Dianne's friend Preston got together with Meri Rosewater in "Psychic Flashes[1]", available everywhere now.

Keep reading for a special except from "Wolf Doctor[2]", book one of the fan-favorite "Bite-Sized Shifters" paranormal romantic comedy series.

---

1. https://books2read.com/u/4ENlDY

2.   https://books2read.com/u/4AOXXK

Special Preview

Wolf Doctor: A Paranormal Romantic Comedy

Twilight. Colt's favorite time of the day.

Stripping off his clothes, he took a deep breath, inhaling the scents in the air. He broke into a run and felt his body change mid-stride. In less than thirty seconds he had transformed from man to wolf.

Muscles and bone lengthening as gray hair sprouted all over his body, almost white in some places. His sharp canine teeth extended from his thickening jaw. He felt his tail grow behind him and he wagged it happily from side to side as he increased his pace, moving so fast his paws seemed to barely touch the ground.

Colt's senses were immediately heightened. His vision was sharper, his ears taking in even the softest sound, and his nose twitched with the wonderful scents of the pristine forest.

He headed through the woods, exhilarating in the feeling of free movement. His wolf loved to run. He hadn't shifted in almost a week. Too long. He needed this. He needed to shift and let his wolf run as much as he needed oxygen or food.

Speaking of food, he could use a snack. He scented a group of hares a mile away and headed in that direction at a gallop. His paws ate up the ground as he tracked the smaller beasts, stopping occasionally to sniff the ground and pick up their trail.

There, up ahead, he saw a flash of fur. He moved quickly, ears pinned back, as his wolf took over, the ultimate predator.

He could smell the fear on the hare as it took off, running for its life. Colt pulled his gums back in a canine smile. He loved the chase. The harder the capture, the better it tasted.

He sped up, following the hare instinctively as it took a sharp turn to the side. He pounced, leaping after the hare. Suddenly his feet hit air. And then he was falling. Fast.

Oh crap. He had overshot and gone right over the edge of the bluff. He could practically feel the stupid hare laughing at him as he tumbled down the embankment, scrambling but unable to stop his downward momentum.

He whined as his body hit the road below with a heavy thump.

Before he could recover he heard the squealing of brakes and suddenly he was airborne again. He landed on the asphalt a second time, feeling bones breaking and muscles tearing. He smelled the scent of his own blood and dimly heard voices as he struggled to stay conscious.

"Oh my god Dennis, you hit that poor dog!" The woman sounded upset.

"I'm not sure that it's a dog Sandy, it might be a wolf," someone, presumably Dennis, responded.

Not a dog, his wolf snipped in his head, clearly offended.

Really, that's your top worry right now? he asked his wolf.

Like all shifters, Colt shared space in his mind with his animal. He and his wolf shared not only the same body, but also the same consciousness.

He noted dimly that the humans who had hit him had exited their truck and were watching him cautiously from where they had stopped. He thought about getting up and whined again. The pain was terrible. It was impossible to move.

"He's bleeding and he's in pain," Sandy said, her voice sounding closer. "We have to get him to the animal hospital."

"There's no way he's going to survive," Dennis answered. "Let me get my shotgun out of the truck and I'll put the poor thing out of his misery."

Colt lifted his head in alarm, although it cost him dearly. He made eye contact with the woman, trying to communicate with her. He tried to make himself look sad and unthreatening. He did not want to die on the side of the road, and he definitely did not want to be put down by some random human with a shotgun. With his luck the guy would be a bad shot and make his injuries even worse.

"NO," Sandy said firmly. "You are not shooting him Dennis. Get the tarp. We'll put him in the back and drive him to the vet."

"He's a wounded animal Sandy," Dennis argued. "He may attack us, especially if he is a wolf."

Sandy continued to hold Colt's gaze. "No, he won't," she replied. "Come on, let's get him some help."

Colt passed out, not knowing who would win their argument. He just hoped it was Sandy.

He did not feel the couple cautiously wrapping him in a tarp and dragging him up into the back of their pick-up. He didn't feel himself sliding around in the truck bed as they raced to the animal hospital. He didn't hear the people loading him onto a gurney and wheeling his large body into the hospital. Both his body and his mind were completely shut down now, blissfully blocking the pain.

Then he felt it. A jolt of happiness and peace.

He opened his eyes, staring through the pain as an angel looked down at him. The overhead light glowed behind her like a halo. Thick brown hair framed her beautiful face. Her eyes were deep brown and impossibly kind.

"What happened?" his angel asked. Her voice made him feel calm. She seemed familiar.

"I think he took a header off a cliff. I think he came rolling down from up above. Suddenly there he was, falling onto the road right in front of us," Dennis explained. "Before I could stop, I hit him with my truck. I didn't do it on purpose, he seemed to come out of nowhere."

The angel's hand dropped gently to his head, rubbing him softly between his ears. He closed his eyes again, pressing against the warmth of her hand and whining softly. He had one thought before he passed out again. *Mate!*

***

For more of Colt and Valerie's story, check out "Wolf Doctor" by Rose Bak. Available now for download[1] at all major online retailers. Binge the whole series today.

1. https://books2read.com/u/4AOXXK

Other Books by Rose Bak

Magical Midlife Series
    Beltane Magic (prequel)
    Love Potion
    Psychic Flashes
    Halloween Surprise
    Giant Love

Bite-Sized Shifters Paranormal Romance Series
    Long Distance Wolf
    Wolf Doctor
    Kat's Dog
    Designer Wolf
    Wolf Sheriff
    Cocktail Wolf
    Second Chance Wolf
    Runaway Wolf

Holidays with the Shifters Series
    Santa's Claws
    Bear Humbug
    Jingle Bear
    Silver Paws
    Joy to the Wolf
    Lion's Heart

Boozy Book Club Series
    Beach Reads
    Bubbly & Billionaires
    Martinis & Mysteries
    Bourbon & Bikers
    Midlife Madness
    Extra Innings

The Good with Numbers Holiday Romance Series

Love Unmasked
The Thanksgiving Scrooge
Maid for Christmas
Countdown to Love
Valentine's Lottery
Christmas Angel
Loving the Holidays Contemporary Romance Series
Dating Santa
New Year's Steve
Independence Dave
Comfort & Joy
Faking It with the Detective
Dropping the Ball
Midlife Crisis Contemporary Romance Series
Summer Wedding
Roasting with Rob
Christmas Punch
Disaster Planning
The Oliver Boys Band Contemporary Romance Series
Until You Came Along
Rock Star Teacher
Rock Star Writer
Rock Star Neighbor
Rock Star Lawyer
The Diamond Bay Contemporary Romance Series
Brand New Penny
Fresh as a Daisy
Right as Rain
Reunited Series
Together Again
Finding My Baby
King of the Reunion

Standalones
Beach Wedding
Jessie's Girl
Factory Reset
Non-fiction
What to Do If You Find a Cougar in Your Living Room: Self-Care in an Uncaring World
It's All About Relationships: Reflections on Love, Friendship, and Connection

Catch up with these and other stories coming soon. Join my newsletter for more information[1] or follow my author page on your favorite retailer.

---

1. *https://storyoriginapp.com/giveaways/62ee758e-068f-11eb-904e-c373f6014fe1*

About the Author

Rose Bak has been obsessed with books since she got her first library card at age five. She is a passionate reader with an e-reader bursting with thousands of beloved books.

Although Rose enjoys writing both fiction and nonfiction, romance novels have always been her favorite guilty pleasure, both as a reader and an author. Rose's contemporary romance books focus on strong female characters over thirty-five and the alpha males who love them. Expect a lot of steam, a little bit of snark, and a guaranteed happily ever after.

Rose lives in the Pacific Northwest with her family, and special needs dogs. In addition to writing, she also teaches accessible yoga and loves music. Sadly, she has absolutely no musical talent, so she mostly sings in the shower.

Please sign up for the Rose Bak Romance newsletter[1] to get a free book and keep up to date on all the latest news. You can also follow Rose on Facebook[2], Instagram[3], Twitter[4], Goodreads[5], or Bookbub[6].

---

1. https://storyoriginapp.com/giveaways/62ee758e-068f-11eb-904e-c373f6014fe1

2. https://www.facebook.com/AuthorRoseBak

3. https://www.instagram.com/authorrosebak/

4. https://twitter.com/AuthorRoseBak

5. https://www.goodreads.com/authorrosebak

6. https://www.bookbub.com/authors/rose-bak

Don't miss out!

Visit the website below and you can sign up to receive emails whenever Rose Bak publishes a new book. There's no charge and no obligation.

https://books2read.com/r/B-A-VATM-DSHIC

Connecting independent readers to independent writers.

Did you love *Giant Love*? Then you should read *Love Potion*[7] by Rose Bak!

[8]

The love spell worked...on the wrong sister!When her sister begs her to do a love spell to attract her true mate, Cami is hesitant. Her magic is glitchy on a good day. But what's the harm of trying? To everyone's shock, the spell manifests exactly the man they hoped for, except for one problem...he's in love with Cami, not her sister.Shapeshifter Stephen doesn't believe in magic, but he does believe in fate. His wolf knows the truth: Cami is his true mate, the one he's destined to be together with forever. If only Cami could forget about the spell and listen to her heart..."Love Potion" is book one in the Magical Midlife Romance series. This steamy opposites attract novella includes matchmaking sisters, a wolf shifter who's found his fated mate, and a little touch of magic

---

7. https://books2read.com/u/4X6pN7

8. https://books2read.com/u/4X6pN7

leading to a sweet happily ever after. Download this instalove romantic comedy today!

Read more at https://rosebakenterprises.com/.